D0633429

Maggie's
Chopsticks

For teachers both in and out of the classroom — A.W.
For my little sunshine, Marianne, and my lovely darling, Alice — I.M.

The Chinese words in the story are
aiya *(eye-YAH)*: expression meaning "oh, no" or "oh, dear"
cha siu bao *(CHAH see-ew ba-ow)*: barbecue pork bun
ha gau *(HAH ga-ow)*: Chinese dumpling

Kids Can Press acknowledges the financial support of the Government of Ontario, through the Ontario Media Development Corporation's Ontario Book Initiative; the Ontario Arts Council; the Canada Council for the Arts; and the Government of Canada, through the BPIDP, for our publishing activity.

Published in Canada by
Kids Can Press Ltd.
25 Dockside Drive
Toronto, ON M5A 0B5

Published in the U.S. by
Kids Can Press Ltd.
2250 Military Road
Tonawanda, NY 14150

www.kidscanpress.com

The artwork in this book was rendered in watercolor and Adobe Photoshop.
The text is set in Mercurius.

Edited by Yvette Ghione
Designed by Marie Bartholomew

This book is smyth sewn casebound.
Manufactured in China, in 3/2012, through Asia Pacific Offset, 3/F, New factory (No.12), Jing Yi Industrial Center, Tian Bei Estate, Fu Ming Community, Guan Lan, Bao An, Shenzhen, China

CM 12 0 9 8 7 6 5 4 3 2 1

Library and Archives Canada Cataloguing in Publication

Woo, Alan, 1977–
Maggie's chopsticks / written by Alan Woo ; illustrated by Isabelle Malenfant.

ISBN 978-1-55453-619-1

I. Malenfant, Isabelle, 1979– II. Title.

PS8645.O47M35 2012 jC813'.6 C2011-906995-4

Kids Can Press is a Corus™ Entertainment company

Written by Alan Woo

Illustrated by Isabelle Malenfant

Kids Can Press

My name is Maggie.

These are my new chopsticks.

Grandmother tells me
I hold my chopsticks the wrong way.
"Do it like me!" she grunts.
Click-clack-clicketing
Her two wooden sticks
With ends burnt black
(And old like her),
She scrabbles for food from the center of the table,
Shoveling rice from bowl to mouth.

"*Aiya*, Maggie!" Mother scolds,
Watching with her eagle eye
At how I hold my chopsticks.
I'm not as swift as her.
Quickly, sharply
She snatches up shrimp,
Making them flip
flop back and forth,
And pops them into her mouth
Like candy.

"That's not how you're supposed to hold chopsticks!"
Brother laughs loudly,
His breath smelling of *cha siu bao* and jasmine tea,
His grip strong and sure.
Bolder than the rest of us,
He plucks the last *ha gau* from the table,
Leaving me hungry
For more.

My chopsticks are awkward and gangly
Like the boys at Sister's high school
Who always blush when she flits by,
Dashing off to ballet class.
"Be graceful like this!" she instructs,
Crossing her chopsticks back and forth,
Back and forth,
Like legs,
Dancing.

"What should I do?"
I ask my cat,
Purring perfectly in my lap.
Mew-Mew yawns, licks his paws
And goes back to sleep.

竈君

The Kitchen God,

Whose picture hangs on the wall,

Just stares back at me

In silence.

"Ancient ancestors,
With your altars, burning incense sticks,
Oranges, Chinese pears
And cups of wine,
What can you tell me
About my chopsticks?"
I ask.
But even they have nothing to say.
So I keep trying.

I hold my chopsticks
Behind my back
Like a magician getting ready
To wow an audience.
But as hard as I try,
I just can't do this magic trick.

I practice under the table
So no one can see.
Two twirling batons
Spinning in secret
And —
OW!
Pinching my fingers.

I circle the chopsticks

Above the fish tank,

Skimming the water.

The fish flee

From the wooden fingers

Reaching through their sky of blue.

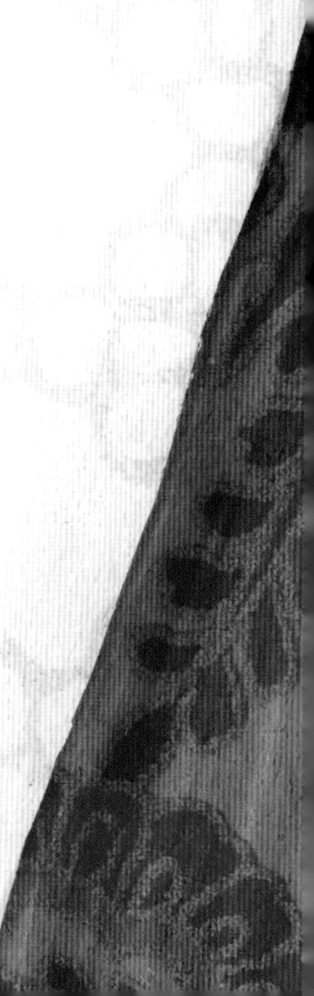

I try the chopsticks in my left hand.
I hold them closer to the top.
Then I hold them near the bottom.
But people still tell me,

"It just isn't right!"

and

"No, not like that!"

But Father says,

"Maggie, you shouldn't worry

What other people think.

Everyone is different.

Everyone is unique."

I handle my chopsticks lightly.

Like a butterfly emerging

From a long winter's sleep,

I am unsure

But ready to fly.

"You hold your chopsticks perfectly,"

Father whispers.

I smile,
Fingers fluttering
Like wings.